Paige Plans It All: Planning Your Perfect Birthday Party!

www.srdharrisbooks.com

Published by S.R.D. Harris Books, LLC and proudly printed in the USA.
Written by: S.R.D. Harris   Illustrated by: Aldila Permata

I am your Perfect Party Planner
and my name is Paige.
Do you want a perfect party
to celebrate your new age?
Everyone knows that my parties
are simply the best!
Let me show you how to plan
your party so you can rest!

To plan your perfect party, you
need to have three parts.
First, decide a theme,
that is where it all starts.
Your theme will dictate
your décor and the
menu for your food.
Be sure to feed your guests so
you are not considered rude.

Choose your very favorite things, anything you really like.

Maybe you
love reading,
cooking,
or riding
your new bike.

Your theme can
even include
things like your
favorite game.

Make your party
as unique to
you as your very
own name.

Before picking out décor,
write down all your favorite hues.

Your perfect party should reflect
the palette that you choose!

Blue or Purple,
Red or Green,
any color will do.

Your favorite color
for your theme
will be perfect for you!

Next, you get to choose
who you want to be there.
List all of your best friends
to be sure you keep it fair.

Do you want a great big party,
or maybe keep it small?
Just a few of your classmates,
or would you rather invite them all?

Now that you have the details set,
let's sprinkle in some fun!

Do you want to play video games
or prefer swimming in the sun?

You get to choose what is best for
you, and what makes you smile.

Your perfect party should make
memories that last for a long while.

How about some music?
Would you like to dance?
Let's pretend you are from
Egypt or the Coast of France!

You could have some quiche,
crepes and gooey cheese fondue.
The options are nearly endless
when I plan your party with you!

What is your favorite sport?
Karate, Soccer or Football?
You can take your friends
outside and enjoy them all!

After playing outside,
you may want to relax.
You can head back inside
and have some tasty snacks.

Do you love to stay up
all night laughing
with your friends?
You could plan
a slumber party,
so the fun never ends!

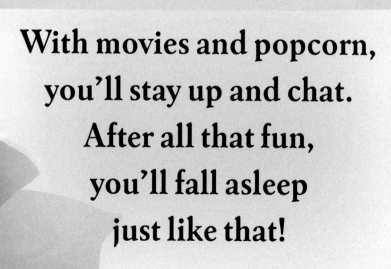

With movies and popcorn,
you'll stay up and chat.
After all that fun,
you'll fall asleep
just like that!

The next morning for breakfast,
you'll have the tastiest treat.

The food is as beautiful as ever,
it's like all-you-can-eat!

It's taller than you, your friends,
and your parents, too!

Everyone will stare and marvel,
as they all say "ooooh!"

Now the hard part is over,
and the party has begun.
Your friends will come to visit
and have lots of fun!

With everything you learned today,
I hope you'll always know.
It's fun to plan a party and
celebrate as you grow!

My Party Ideas

Date & Time

_____

Theme & Colors

_____

_____

Food & Fun

_____

_____

_____

Family & Friends

_____

_____

_____

_____

_____

_____

_____

srdharrisbooks.com

My To-Do List

_____

_____

_____

_____

_____

_____

srdharrisbooks.com

This book is dedicated to my amazing husband and our three wonderful daughters!

Thank you for your constant support, love, and encouragement!

Special thanks to my Co-Author, Camryn, who helps me with all of my books!

To readers and party lovers everywhere-keep celebrating yourself

and always stay true to what makes **YOU** unique!

To my wonderful friends and family, thank you for your tremendous support!

In loving memory of my first hero and best friend, my Daddy, T. E. Harris.

Visit srdharrisbooks.com to learn about all of our uplifting books!

Please be sure to like, share and REVIEW our books!